P9-CDK-678

JOURNEY TO **STAR WARS: THE RISE OF SKYWALKER**

STAR WARS™

RESISTANCE HEROES

WRITTEN BY MICHAEL SIGLAIN

ILLUSTRATED BY DIOGO SAITO & LUIGI AIMÉ

DISNEP

LUCASFILM
PRESS

LOS ANGELES · NEW YORK

© & TM 2019 Lucasfilm Ltd.

All rights reserved. Published by Disney • Lucasfilm Press, an imprint of Disney Book Group. No part of this book may be reproduced or transmitted in any form or by any means, electronic or mechanical, including photocopying, recording, or by any information storage and retrieval system, without written permission from the publisher. For information address Disney • Lucasfilm Press, 1200 Grand Central Avenue, Glendale, California 91201.

Printed in the United States of America

First Edition, October 2019   10 9 8 7 6 5 4 3 2 1

Library of Congress Control Number on file

FAC-029261-19225

ISBN 978-1-368-05245-0

Visit the official *Star Wars* website at: www.starwars.com.

If you purchased this book without a cover, you should be aware that this book is stolen property. It was reported as "unsold and destroyed" to the publisher, and neither the author nor the publisher has received any payment for this "stripped" book.

A long time ago
in a galaxy far, far away,
there was peace.
Until . . .

. . . the First Order
attacked!

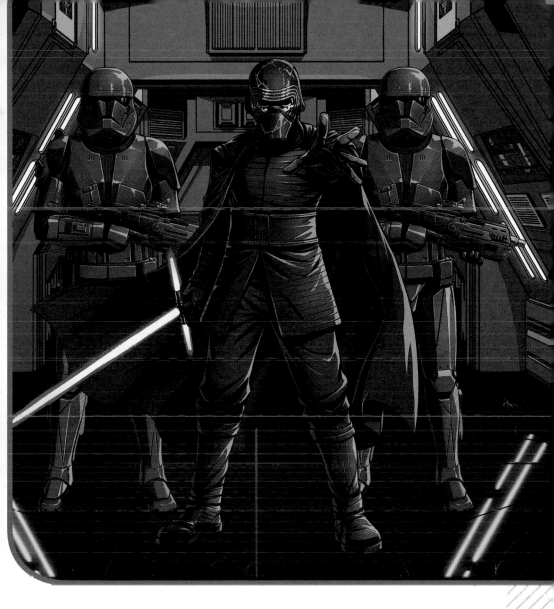

The evil First Order,
led by the dark warrior Kylo Ren,
wants to rule over all.

But the heroes of the Resistance
want to stop the First Order.

The Resistance fights to
bring freedom to the galaxy.

General Leia Organa
is the leader of the Resistance.
Leia is strong, wise, and brave.

Many years ago, Leia fought against
Darth Vader and the evil Empire.
Now Leia fights against
Kylo Ren and the First Order.

Poe Dameron is the best pilot
in the Resistance.

Poe flies a special X-wing fighter
with his loyal droid, BB-8.

Rey is from the desert planet Jakku.

Rey once helped save BB-8.

Then she joined the Resistance.

Rey is strong in the Force.

The Force is a mystical energy field
that binds the galaxy together.

Finn used to fight for the First Order.

He was a stormtrooper.

But Finn did not like
fighting for the First Order.
So he joined the Resistance instead.

R2-D2 and C-3PO are droids.

R2-D2 is brave.

C-3PO is not.

But together, R2-D2 and C-3PO

make a good team.

Many years ago, R2-D2 and C-3PO
helped Leia fight
against the Empire.
Now these droids help Leia
fight against the First Order.

Chewbacca, also known as Chewie,
is a furry Wookiee.
He is the copilot of a fast ship
called the *Millennium Falcon*.

Chewie is over 200 years old.

He is strong and kind.

Chewie has fought against the Empire
and the First Order for many years.

Others have joined in the fight
against the First Order, too.

D-O is a curious roller droid
who never leaves BB-8's side.

And Jannah leads a group of
brave warriors from an ocean moon.

Together, the Resistance has
fought the First Order
in dangerous space battles . . .

. . . and in epic ground battles.

But to truly stop the First Order, Rey will have to defeat Kylo Ren. Rey will fight Kylo Ren with a lightsaber.

Lightsabers are the weapons
of the noble Jedi and the evil Sith.
Rey learned to use a lightsaber
by training with Leia's brother—
Jedi Master Luke Skywalker.

Many years ago, Luke fought
against Darth Vader
and the evil Empire.
Together, Luke, Leia, and the rebels
stopped Vader and saved the galaxy.

Years later, after training Rey,
Luke gave his life
to save the Resistance.

Now, with BB-8 by her side,
Rey continues
her Jedi training.